THE NOT-SO SECRET SOCIETY™

TALE OF THE GUMMY

ROSS RICHIE CEO & Founder • MATT GAGNON Editor-in-Chief • FILIP SABLIK President of Publishing & Marketing • STEPHEN CHRISTY President of Development • LANCE KREITER VP of Licensing & Merchandising
PHIL BARBARO VP of Finance • ARUNE SINGH VP of Marketing • BRYCE CARLSON Managing Editor • MEL CAYLO Marketing Manager • SCOTT NEWMAN Production Design Manager • KATE HENNING Operations Manager
SIERRA HAHN Senior Editor • DAFNA PLEBAN Editor, Talent Development • SHANNON WATTERS Editor • ERIC HARBURN Editor • WHITNEY LEOPARD Editor • JASMINE AMIRI Editor • CHRIS ROSA Associate Editor • ALEX GALER Associate Editor
CAMERON CHITTOCK Associate Editor • MATTHEW LEVINE Assistant Editor • SOPHIE PHILIPS-ROBERTS Assistant Editor • KELSEY DIETERICH Designer • JILLIAN CRAB Production Designer • MICHELLE ANKLEY Production Designer
KARA LEOPARD Production Designer • GRACE PARK Production Design Assistant • ELIZABETH LOUGHRIDGE Accounting Coordinator • STEPHANIE HOCUTT Social Media Coordinator • JOSÉ MEZA Event Coordinator
JAMES ARRIOLA Mailroom Assistant • HOLLY AITCHISON Operations Assistant • MEGAN CHRISTOPHER Operations Assistant • MORGAN PERRY Direct Market Representative • AMBER PARKER Administrative Assistant

Macrocosm Entertainment, Inc. ®

MACROCOSM®
Trevor Crafts CEO & Founder
Ellen Scherer Crafts COO
Matthew Daley VP of Development

THE NOT-SO SECRET SOCIETY, July 2017. Published by KaBOOM!, a division of Boom Entertainment, Inc. THE NOT-SO
SECRET SOCIETY is ™ & © 2017 Macrocosm Entertainment, Inc.™ All rights reserved. KaBOOM!™ and the KaBOOM! logo
are trademarks of Boom Entertainment, Inc., registered in various countries and categories. All characters, events, and
institutions depicted herein are fictional. Any similarity between any of the names, characters, persons, events, and/or
institutions in this publication to actual names, characters, and persons, whether living or dead, events, and/or institutions
is unintended and purely coincidental. KaBOOM! does not read or accept unsolicited submissions of ideas, stories, or artwork.

BOOM! Studios, 5670 Wilshire Boulevard, Suite 450, Los Angeles, CA 90036-5679. Printed in China. First Printing.

ISBN: 978-1-60886-997-8, eISBN: 978-1-61398-668-4

COVER BY
Wook Jin Clark

DESIGNER
Kara Leopard

ASSISTANT EDITOR
Matthew Levine

EDITOR
Whitney Leopard

SPECIAL THANKS
Stephen Silver
Matthew Sugarman
Mary Gumport
Shannon Watters

THE NOT-SO SECRET SOCIETY ™

CREATED BY
Matthew Daley, Arlene Daley,
Trevor Crafts, Ellen Crafts

WRITTEN BY
Matthew & Arlene Daley

ILLUSTRATED BY
Wook Jin Clark

COLORS BY
Eleonora Bruni

LETTERS BY
Warren Montgomery

"MINI COMICS"

WRITTEN BY
Matthew & Arlene Daley

ILLUSTRATED BY

Rachel Dukes	Nichole Matthews
Kat Leyh	Zachary Sterling
Nicole Mannino	Kiernan Sjursen-Lien
Wook Jin Clark	Pranas Naujokaitis
Katie Cook	Meg Omac
Jorge Corona	Jay Fosgitt
Eva Cabrera	Rii Abrego
Mad Rupert	Fred C. Stresing
Kelly Matthews	Meg Casey

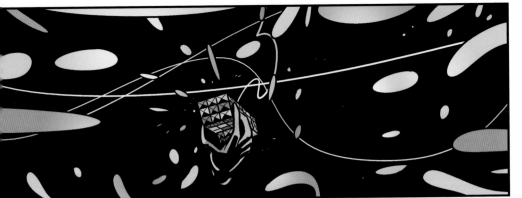

CHARGED IN LESS THAN TWO SECONDS.

100%

BEST CLASS PROJECT. *EVER.* OH. AND IT MIGHT CHANGE THE WORLD TOO.

IT TAKES RECYCLABLE ITEMS, LIKE BOTTLES, CANS, AND PAPER, AND TURNS THEM INTO USEFUL CLASSROOM TOOLS.

DOUBLE EWWW!

LET'S SHOW THESE CLOWNS HOW IT WORKS.

FIRE IT UP!!!

TODAY, WE'RE MAKING PAPER.

INFINITY EWWW!!!

THIS IS "PAPER OF THE FUTURE".

WE'RE SUBMITTING SOMETHING!

WE ARE?!

THE NOT-SO SECRET SOCIETY. IT'S NO SECRET THAT YOU *LOVE* TO EMBARRASS YOURSELVES.

MM-HMM. GOOD LUCK WITH YOUR LITTLE PROJECT.

LUCK?! WE DON'T NEED LUCK!

YOU'RE RIGHT. YOU DON'T NEED LUCK. YOU NEED A *MIRACLE*.

I LOVE WHEN PEOPLE GET EXCITED ABOUT SCIENCE!

REMEMBER, WE'RE SCIENTISTS, NOT PRO WRESTLERS.

WE CAN'T LET OUR EMOTIONS GET THE BEST OF US.

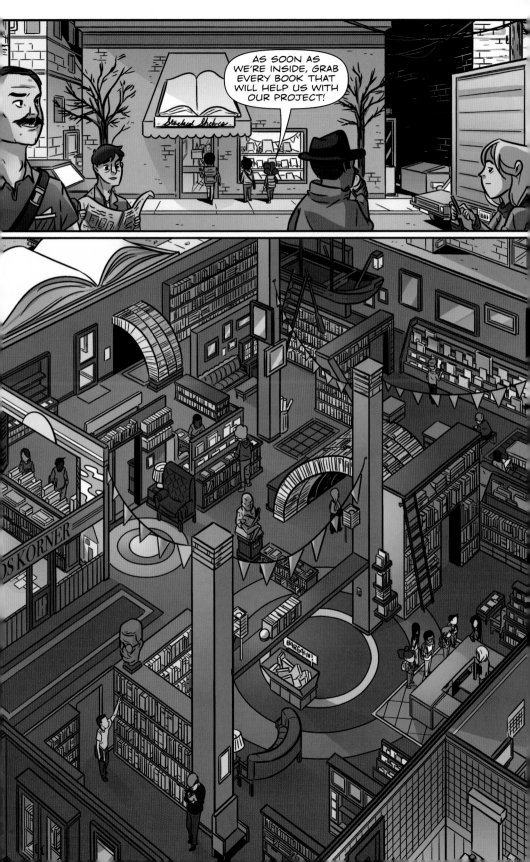

VUMLEE CANDIES CLOSED

On Halloween Day to Sponsor Extravaganza at High-Five Towers.

I'D LOVE TO HAVE CANDY FRIENDS.

AND IF ANY OF THESE CANDIES ACT UP, I'LL PUT THEM IN THE GRIZZLY JAW SUBMISSION.

WE SHOULD TAKE THIS TOO. JUST IN CASE.

WE WON'T NEED IT!

JUST IN CASE.

KNOWING US, WE'LL DEFINITELY NEED IT.

I CAN'T WAIT TILL TOMORROW.

I'M GOING TO EAT CANDY TILL MY TEETH FALL OUT.

HALLOWEEN ☠ EXTRAVAGANZA!

High Five
Towers

I HAVE TO FINISH MAKING MY COSTUME.

ME TOO! IT'S THE SAME AS LAST YEAR, ONLY DIFFERENT.

MINE IS A WORK OF ART THIS YEAR.

BEFORE WE GET ALL HOPPED-UP ON HALLOWEEN, WE SHOULD BUILD OUR SCIENCE FAIR PROJECT.

THIS WILL CHANGE THE WORLD OF SCIENCE FOREVER.

HE NEEDS A NAME.

AT LEAST HE'S SMALL. HE CAN'T REALLY BREAK ANYTHING.

SHOULD CANDY EAT CANDY?

LOOK!

UMM...

WHAT HAVE WE DONE?!?

RELAX DYLAN. EVERYTHING IS UNDER CONTROL.

WE'LL KEEP HIM AWAY FROM SUGAR.

I'LL KEEP GUMMY AT MY HOUSE THIS WEEKEND.

THERE'S *NEVER* ANY CANDY IN MY HOUSE. EVEN ON HALLOWEEN.

HE SHOULD COME TO THE HALLOWEEN EXTRAVAGANZA WITH US.

HE'D GO PERFECTLY WITH MY COSTUME.

WE'VE GOT TO BE SMART ABOUT THIS.

WE ARE! MY HOUSE IS TH SAFEST PLACE TO KEEP GUMMY.

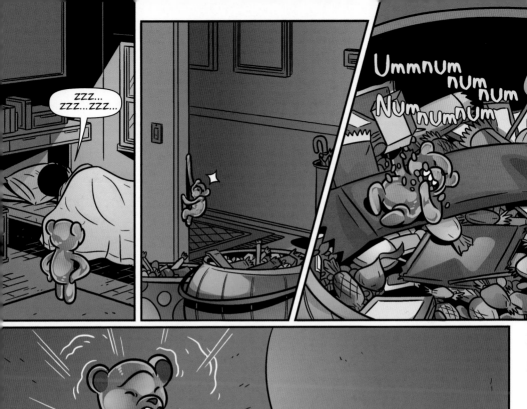

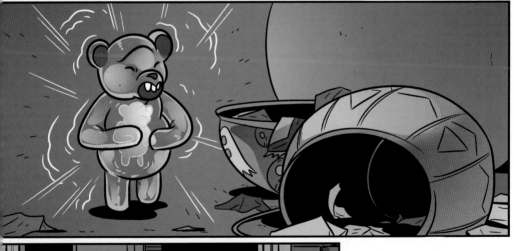

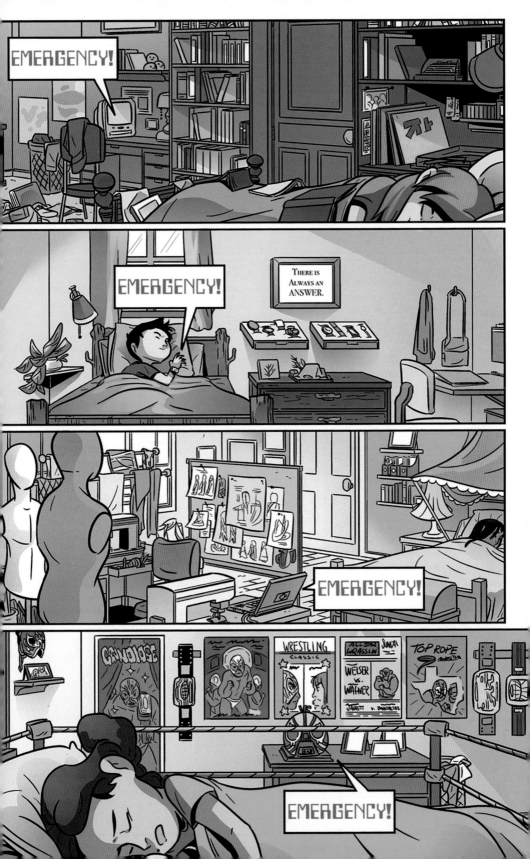

Saturday, October 31st

THIS BETTER BE IMPORTANT.

REAL IMPORTANT.

GUMMY ESCAPED!

YOU SAID IT WAS SAFE HERE!

I KNEW THIS WOULD HAPPEN.

I KNOW THIS IS MY FAULT. BUT I DIDN'T THINK HE WOULD ESCAPE!

THIS IS WHY WE SHOULD HAVE BUILT THE CANDY DREAM.

MM-HMM.

YOU ATE ALL THE CANDY APPLES!

WHAT ARE YOU TALKING ABOUT?!!?

MR. JEFFERSON DIDN'T EAT THE CANDY APPLES!

EXACTLY! I DON'T LIKE CANDY APPLES.

WAIT-- WHO ARE YOU AND WHAT ARE YOU DOING HERE?

WE'RE THE NOT-SO SECRET SOCIETY. OUR FRIEND ATE YOUR APPLES.

I'M 108% SURE WE'LL FIND HIM!

WHEN WE DO, WE'LL BRING YOU BACK YOUR APPLES!

KIDS NOWADAYS ARE SO STRANGE.

WAIT!

HEY... AGAIN. STILL LOVE THE COSTUMES!

HE'S NOT HERE.

THERE!

Umm num num Umm num Num num num

LET ME AT HIM!

THANKS FOR THE HELP.

YOU SAID YOU COULD HOLD HIM!

HE'S ONLY A PIECE OF CANDY!

WHO WANTED TO BRING CANDY TO LIFE? NOT ME!

AND THAT "PIECE OF CANDY" IS CRAZY STRONG.

HOW CAN WE STOP GUMMY IF AVA CAN'T HOLD HIM?

WHAT IF WE CAN'T STOP HIM?

TERROR
AVENUE

YOU MUST BE
THIS
TALL

THE MIXTURE HAS TO BE STRONG.

DENTISTS SHOULD USE THESE.

ALMOST DONE.

WHERE DO WE THINK GUMMY MIGHT BE?

WELL, HE LOVES SUGAR.

THAT NARROWS IT DOWN TO EVERY BOOTH.

IF I WERE GUMMY, I'D VISIT THE CARAMEL CORN WHEEL, ICE CREAM DIP, AND COTTON CANDY TIME.

WE SHOULD STICK TOGETHER. JUST IN CASE HE'S SUPER-DUPER BIG BY NOW.

WHAT IF HE'S ESCAPED HIGH-FIVE TOWERS?

WE'LL HAVE TO CALL IN A TEAM THAT FIGHTS GHOSTS, ALIENS, AND GIANT CANDY.

NO NEED. THAT'S WHAT WE'RE GONNA' DO!

WE DON'T NEED TO FIND A BIG CANDY BAR.

WE HAVE YOU!

I CAN'T GO UP THERE!

OF COURSE YOU CAN! GUMMY *LOVES* LIPPER'S LICORICE.

WHAT ARE YOU GOING TO DO WHEN I'M UP THERE?

WE'LL SET A TRAP IN TOWER FIVE! IT'S STILL UNDER CONSTRUCTION. NOBODY'S THERE.

I'M NOT *REAL* LICORICE!

Tower Five Coming Next Summer

YOU HAD TO WEAR A CANDY COSTUME, DIDN'T YOU?

YOU'RE SAFE!

DID YOU ALREADY CATCH GUMMY?

THIS IS ALL OUR FAULT.

WE BUILT A MACHINE THAT BRINGS CANDY TO LIFE.

IT WAS A BAD IDEA.

A BAD IDEA?

THIS IS THE FUTURE OF CANDY!

THIS IS THE MOST EXCITING HALLOWEEN EXTRAVAGANZA EVER!

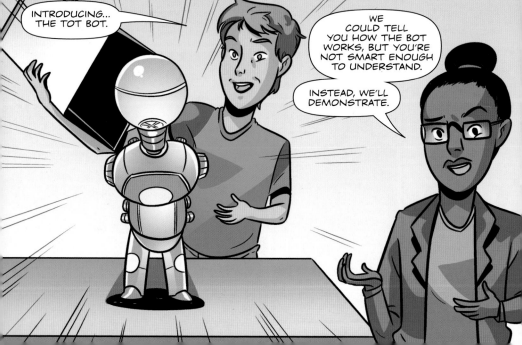

AFTER CAREFUL DELIBERATIONS, THE TEAM THAT WILL BE REPRESENTING US AT THE ALL-CITY SCIENCE FAIR IS...

THE 5Z'S!

WE CAN TRY AGAIN NEXT YEAR.

OR JUST INVENT STUFF FOR OURSELVES.

MS. DOUGLASS! YOU'RE WHO I WANT TO BE WHEN I GROW UP.

THANKS! YOUR CANDY DREAM IS QUITE A MACHINE.

I LIKED YOURS BEST.

THE FIVE OF YOU SHOULD VISIT ME AT THE NATURAL HISTORY MUSEUM.

I'D LOVE TO HEAR ABOUT SOME OF YOUR "REAL" INVENTIONS.

MINI COMICS

WRITTEN BY
Matthew & Arlene Daley

LETTERED BY
Warren Montgomery

1 Illustrated by
Wook Jin Clark
Colors by
Jeremy Lawson

2 Illustrated by
Jorge Corona
Colors by
Laura Langston

3 Illustrated & Lettered by
Kat Leyh

4 Illustrated by
Kelly & Nichole Matthews

5 Illustrated by
Mad Rupert
Colors by
Laura Langston

6 Illustrated by
Eva Cabrera

7 Illustrated & Lettered by
Kat Leyh

8 Illustrated by
Rachel Dukes

9 Illustrated by
Nikki Mannino
Colors by
Laura Langston

10 Illustrated by
Katie Cook
Colors by
Eleonora Bruni

11 Illustrated by
Jorge Corona
Colors by
Jeremy Lawson

12 Illustrated by
Mad Rupert
Colors by
Laura Langston

13 Illustrated by
Eva Cabrera

14 Illustrated & Lettered by
Kat Leyh

15 Illustrated by
Fred C. Stresing &
Meg Casey

16 Illustrated & Lettered by
Rii Abergo

17 Illustrated by
Kiernan Sjursen-Lien
Colors by
Eleonora Bruni

18 Illustrated & Lettered by
Kat Leyh

19 Illustrated by
Eva Cabrera

20 Illustrated by
Zachary Sterling
Colors by
Jeremy Lawson

21 Illustrated & Lettered by
Pranas Naujokaitis
Colors by
Jeremy Lawson

22 Illustrated & Lettered by
Meg Omac

23 Illustrated by
Eva Cabrera

24 Illustrated by
Jay Fosgitt
Colors by
Eleonora Bruni

25 Illustrated & Lettered by
Pranas Naujokaitis
Colors by
Jenna Ayoub

*Moi•e•ty (noun): One of two equal parts.

HOW IT ALL STARTED

When we began developing The Not-So Secret Society, we set out to create a project for kids that was inspired by the great stories we loved when we were young. We wanted something that sent positive messages to readers and, of course, something that was really, really fun.

We used our vast experience as parents, educators, and world-builders, to develop a project that both kids and the adults in their lives will love. In the Not-So Secret Society we encourage:

EMBRACING OF DIFFERENCES

SPIRIT OF ADVENTURE

SENSE OF COLLABORATION

EXPLORATION & LEARNING

RESPECT FOR ADULTS

So once we had the basics down, we worked with concept illustrator Stephen Silver to bring the characters to life. But it takes more than one person to bring an idea to the printed page. The Kids of the NS3 evolved and grew.

Original Stephen Silver Sketch

we took it to our friends at BOOM! Studios. They believed in our vision and helped to make it the great book that you just read with the help of Wook Jin Clark, an incredible artist, who really added a great dynamic to the NS3.

As parents and educators we wanted to give you more than just a book. We know you're always looking for that special series to share with the kids in your life. Something that you trust and your kids will love. So we've created activities for our young readers to partake in at home or at school. For all the teachers out there, the lesson plans align to the Common Core Standards and they are always free for everyone on our website:

www.TeamNS3.com/parents-educators

Thank you for joining us – and The Not-So Secret Society – on this incredible journey. There are a few activities and lesson plans on the next few pages to get you started. We are looking forward to bringing you many more adventures!

Matt Daley   Arlene Daley   Trevor Crafts   Ellen Crafts

PARENT READING GUIDE

BEFORE YOU READ

1. Based on the title, "The Not-So Secret Society: Tale of the Gummy", what do you expect the story to be about?

2. There's something BIG behind the "Caution/Keep Out" yellow tape. What do you think it is? Should the kids be afraid? Why/why not?

AFTER YOU READ

3. Ava volunteers the NS3 to compete in the All-City Science Fair. Should she have discussed it with her friends first? Why/why not?

4. The NS3 decide NOT to tell anyone else about Gummy. Do you think that was the right decision? Who do you think they should have told and how would that have potentially helped?

5. The NS3 lose the All-City Science Fair to the 5Z's. Do you think they deserved to win? Why/why not?

6. The NS3 will certainly have more adventures in the future. What do you think they learned from "Tale of the Gummy"? What mistakes won't they make in the future?

ADVENTURE HUNT ACTIVITY

HOW TO PLAY

The Not-So Secret Society have quite an adventure trying to track down Gummy in The Not-So Secret Society: Tale of the Gummy. Now you and your kids can create your own exciting Adventure Hunt with these simple steps. No matter the weather, all you'll need is a location and some imagination!

How to play:

1. Determine your game area and create boundaries. Think about places like a bedroom, basement, or backyard.

2. Come up with items that you would like to hide. Popular options are toys, clothing items, school supplies (pen/pencil), books, food, utensils.

3. Find sneaky places to hide your items. Don't make the hiding places too easy!

4. Create a time limit depending on your child's age and ability.

5. Provide the player(s) with Adventure Hunt clue sheets to help them find the items.

6. Every player is a winner! At the end of the game, reward your child with something special.

Find a sample Adventure Hunt, including printable clue sheets, on the Parent Page of our website, along with other great activities:

www.TeamNS3.com/parents-educators

OUR GREEN EARTH LESSON

Subject: Science, Art - Common Core Alignment
CCSS.ELA-LITERACY.RF.3.4.A

Objectives & Outcomes
Students will learn about the importance of recycling, upcycling, and how to creatively promote recycling.

Materials Needed
Recycling Facts Handout, (available on www.teamns3.com/parents-educators), Art Supplies, (crayons, colored pencils, scissors, paper, paint, etc.) Various Recyclable items, (bottles, containers, etc.) Poster Board.

Opening
Students will learn the difference between: Recycling (converting waste into reusable materials) and Upcycling (reuse discarded objects or materials in such a way as to create a product of a higher quality or value than the original). Teacher will ask students to share their experiences with recycling for a short discussion. Think about the ways that kids may recycle or upcycle and have them explain.

Questions: What are different ways that people recycle? Would that be considered upcycling? Ex: soda bottle into fleece sweatshirts/reusable grocery bags.

Students will learn briefly some important facts about Recycling and how an absence of Recycling can damage the environment in short term and long term ways. The reading will be guided; handout will be provided to all students.

Group Work
Students will work in teams to create a poster board with a focus on one type of recycling they would like people to do. Teacher will give examples such as: printer cartridges, textiles (clothing), batteries, bottles, paper, electronics, etc. They must include at least one fact about recycling, a slogan, and one of the recyclable items on their poster board. The teacher will encourage them to be as creative as possible within the parameters established. The teacher will move throughout the room to work with each group, to help solve any issues and assure that the students are working properly on the task.

Closing
Groups will present their posters to the entire class. The teacher will allow for the spectator groups to offer positive comments to the presenting group. Once finished, groups will hang their posters inside or outside the classroom for display.

CHARACTERIZATION LESSON

Subject: English/Language Arts - Common Core Alignment
CCSS.ELA-LITERACY.RL.3.3

Objectives & Outcomes
Students will be able to understand how the heroes are characterized and how that enriches the story.

Materials Needed
The Not-So Secret Society: Tale of the Gummy,
Character Charts (available at www.teamns3.com/parents-educators), Poster Board.

Opening
Students will receive a sample Character Chart to introduce them to the vocabulary terms (Traits, What They Say, Actions, Feelings). For the demonstration, students will fill out the Character Chart based on themselves.

Group Work
Students will be provided with five Character Charts, one for each of the heroes from the book. The teacher will place students in five groups. All the groups will work together to fill out the Character Charts for each character, using the book to support their work. The teacher will work with each group, to provide guidance and insight, and assure that students are basing their responses on what they find in the text (and not solely on memory).

Presentations
The teacher will hang five poster board-sized Character Charts on the front board, one per hero from the book. Each group will be assigned one character to present to the class. As groups present, they will fill-in the poster board-sized Character Chart. After each group presents, the spectator groups will be able to add any elements they deem important to the other groups' Character Charts.

Closing
To assure that students understand the importance of Characterization, the teacher will lead students through a writing exercise, pertaining to the main characters:

What do you think a specific character would do in another situation, like: dealing with a bully, a problem they didn't know how to solve, or getting in trouble for something they didn't do?

Have the students answer the prompt and write a short answer in a writing journal They will then share out and discuss the importance of characterization.

ABOUT THE TEAM

ARLENE worked as an educator for over 10 years and she always had a love for storytelling. As a kid, she was an avid fan of *The Babysitters Club*, *Sweet Valley High*, and *Nancy Drew* and used to spend her free time after school writing short stories for her friends & family, dreaming that she would one day write books. Besides raising 3 kids and writing with her husband Matthew, she is always on the hunt for gummy bears.

ELLEN began reading at an early age. As she grew up she was lucky enough to have boxes from her mom of empowering classic girl's adventure and mystery series' like *Nancy Drew*, *Cherry Ames* and *Trixie Belden*. Her career led her into the the world of marketing and events and then entertainment, where she works with her husband Trevor building worlds like those she likes to read about. She is currently compiling a box of books for their toddler daughter to enjoy when she is ready.

MATTHEW was 5 when he wanted to be a member of The Goonies, when he was 9, he wanted to be the fifth member of the Teenage Mutant Ninja Turtles, and when he was 12, he wanted to be in the X-Men. As an adult, he discovered that it's a lot more fun creating a cool team instead of joining an old one. He spent over 10 years working in education before writing full-time. When he and Arlene aren't writing together, they're raising their 3 kids.

TREVOR was a world builder from the very start. Taking his toys and creating elaborate universes and storylines was a daily activity in Trevor's boyhood home. He always loved the stories and books his Father read him, everything from the *Chronicles of Narnia* and the *Dark is Rising* to the *Indian in the Cupboard*. Now Trevor has the best job ever and gets to create worlds like those and share them with everyone.

WOOK loves to read manga, drink lots and lots of coffee and watch wrestling when he isn't drawing awesome books like *The Not-So Secret Society*, *Megagogo*, *The Return of the King*, *Adventure Time*, and *Regular Show*.